Getting Used to the Dark

Getting Used to the Dark

26 Night Poems
by Susan Marie Swanson

illustrated by Peter Catalanotto

A RICHARD JACKSON BOOK

DK Publishing, Inc.

New York

A DK INK BOOK

2 4 6 8 10 9 7 5 3 1

DK Publishing, Inc.

95 Madison Avenue

New York, NY 10016

Visit us on the World Wide Web at http://www.dk.com

Manufactured in the United States of America.

Printed and bound by Berryville Graphics.

The text of this book is set in 14 point Fournier.

The illustrations for the poems, drawn with primary pencil, are
fragments of the single piece of art reproduced on pages 46–47.

Library of Congress cataloging is available upon request.

ISBN 0-7894-2468-1

For Tom—S.M.S

For Megan—P.C.

Contents

Names for Night

1. *Girl*

Night makes mischief,
taunting the wind.
When she comes running
through the swishing willow trees,
I see her books,
her jacket, her shoes,
all covered with wild leaves
and stars.

2. Spider

Night spins webs
everywhere—
in dark doorways,
on shadowy sidewalks,
across the whole sky.
I'm trying to get to sleep.
My math homework
and the names of explorers
are all tangled up
in the web inside my head.

3. Boat

Good thing the moon has a light
so she can read her map
and find the ropes and rudder
to sail this big black boat called Night
over every ocean, stream,
and puddle
on Earth.

Trouble, Fly

Trouble, fly
out of our house.
We left the window
open for you.

Fly like smoke from a chimney.
Fly like the whistle from a train.
Fly far, far
away from my family,
mumbling in their sleep.

Trouble, fly.
Let our night
be a night of peace.

Night Lights

The stars are hard to tell apart,
and so are the square lights
lined up in rows
on big buildings.
Buses are rumbling houses of light.
Words filled with light
flash on, flash off,
pretending to know something.
The headlights of cars
light up the rain
before it hits the street.

Night Knows

Where is it going, the train on the bridge?
And the wail of the whistle?
Where do the bees go at night?
And the glow of the bees?
Who built the house in my dream?
Why does the light inside
stop at the glass?

Nick and the Stale Bread

When Nick finishes his homework,
his head hurts, and rain clatters
on the cold night window.
Grandma says,
"Want to make French toast?"
Nick shrugs.
They cut slices of old bread
into triangles and squares.
Nick still has a scowl on his face,
from spelling words and rain
and his mom out of town for her job.
Outside, it's starting to sleet.
This is like that old story
where some strangers tell the villagers
they can make soup from stones.
The only thing on the table
is a plate of stale bread,

but then Nick cracks the eggs,
and they glow like sunlight
in the night house.
When he whisks the eggs,
some of their light
gets into his thoughts.
Grandma pours the milk.
Nick tells her about the time
he watched a new butterfly open its wings.
While the bread sizzles on the griddle,
out come cinnamon, syrup,
and more stories
to warm up the chilly house.
Nick picks up a shiny fork.
Though he hasn't taken a bite yet,
the night tastes sweet.

Joanie Ice-skating After Dark

Here is Joanie by the rattling heater
lacing up her skates.
She tugs at the laces
until her fingers tingle.
When she wobbles onto the ice,
she pretends

the warming house is her cabin
and the city lights
are northern lights and shooting stars.
Some of the skaters are really reindeer;
some are bears.

Joanie is a robber girl with a sooty cape!
A robber girl who pinches her mother!
A robber girl who catches fish
through a hole in the ice
and roasts them over the fire on sticks!

When she tumbles into a drift,
at the edge of the rink,
snow sifts into her mittens,
and the wind tries
to break into her heart.
The robber girl doesn't mind the cold.
She'll skate all night,
but it's time for Joanie
to untie her skates
and go home.

Truck of Dreams

There is a truck in my mind,
and the driver has a magic map
that unfolds and unfolds
and unfolds until it is as big as a house.
The truck is loaded with boxes
full of dreams.

There are horses galloping
in one of the boxes.
When they stop to drink
and tear at the grass,
they make big shadows.
The horses in my dream
are stronger than the wind.

There is a box of clouds,
and another box with echoes in it.
There are golden candles
in one box, made from the wax
that bees make,
and there is a box of buzzing bees,
and a box filled
with every kind of flower
in the world.

To Be Like the Sun

1. *Spring*

Hello, little seed,
striped gray seed.
Do you really know everything
about sunflowers?
My hoe breaks apart
the clods of brown earth,
but you do the real work
down in the dark.
Not radish work or pumpkin,
not thistle work—
sunflower work.
All the instructions
are written in your heart.

2. Summer

Sunflower,
I heard the rain chatter
to all the seeds underground.
Were you listening?
I didn't hear you say
anything back.
When you found your way
out of the ground,
you looked hard at the sun.
You made roots and leaves,
then stem,
more leaves,
more roots,
stem,
and now
you've made your own sun
up over my head.

3. *Autumn*

The whole world wants to be golden
like you, Sunflower,
to rest in the cool air
after sunset,
looking at the place
where the sun went down,
thinking about the sun
even when it has gone away.

4. *Winter*

The wind rattles
in the garden, tattering
dead leaves and stems.
Cold wind rocks our bird feeder
filled with little seeds,
striped gray sunflower seeds.
Sunflower,
we taped a snapshot of you
to our refrigerator.
Your picture
is smaller than my hand,
and a sunflower seed
is smaller than a word,
but I remember:
you were taller than everyone.
When the winter sky shivers
with icy stars,
I remember how hard you worked
to be like the sun.

Gold in My Thoughts

I wish I had a blanket made of sun.
When Winter rattles windows,
I wish I had a blanket spun from straw
or summer sand.
With a blanket made of dandelions,
I'd never get cold.
When Winter rattles windows
in the frosty night,
dreams are my golden crown.

Poem to Bring a Good Dream

Dream where the moon ripples on the river.
Dream a place where pear trees bloom.
Dream a flashlight beam on the path.
Dream the swish of grass.

Poetry Dream

We met Poetry
where rough grass sprang
out of the water,
where the sun was about to come up.

She was paddling her canoe
out of the lake into a marsh
filled with birds.

Poetry was a red-haired girl
wearing her grandpa's old cap.
She was singing about tea
and cocoa, but she had cold water

to drink, stored in a canteen
of shiny steel that rings
when it falls on a rock.

My Heart Is a Cricket

My heart is a cricket
singing to the other crickets
with its wings.
My thoughts are sparrows
hopping after crumbs.
My voice is made
from scraps of paper and clouds.
My mind has a tornado in it
and a harmonica man,
and a whole city
under the moon.
My wishes prickle like pine needles,
flicker like stars.

Karla's Worries

Karla's scissors are lost.
Math homework not done.
The ivy plant on the windowsill
wants water.

Night has broken the city
into bits and pieces of light,

and the lights say,
Wait for the sun.

Can't remember Dad's new phone number.
Can't miss the bus again.
Can't sleep.

The scattered bits of light say,
Wait for the sun.

Need to get Momma a birthday present.
Where is that missing glove?
Pillowcase torn.
Shoelace snapped.

They won't—
or will they?
Will they wait?

The bits and pieces of light say,
Wait for the sun.

What Happened

I used to be afraid
to cross my room in the dark,
but when I did,
my fear turned into a map
for tracking bears.

At the piano recital
I didn't want to play that polka,
but when I played it,
my shyness turned to streamers
shimmering through the air.

When my parents gave my dog away,
my anger was a piece of crumpled paper.
I smoothed that paper out
and put it between the pages of a book
inside my mind.

Getting Used to the Dark

I like getting used to the dark,
looking and looking
at the blank air
until I can read my hands
in front of my face.

I decided to write a poem
about getting used to the dark.
I clicked off the light.
I started writing shadow words on a piece
of shadow paper
with a shadow pencil.
While I was writing,
the paper got lighter
and lighter,
and the words got darker,
until I could see what I know.

Summer Sleep Charm

When the fan whirs in the window
and a little breeze whispers through the heat,
we are peaceful.

When the refrigerator hums
to the ice cubes and cold milk,

and the tags on the dog's collar clink
while he finds a cooler place on the floor,
we are peaceful.

When the crickets
play and play their summer song,
we are peaceful.
We have peaceful sleep.

Telescope Poem

Telescope,
I hope
you help me get a big wish
from that star.

Night House

When cars go past my window,
the headlights hit my bedroom wall
like big strokes of paint
that disappear.

Outside, the trees look black and gray.
Below my window, where I can't see,
there is a plant
with flowers shaped like bells.

I can hear my brother clicking his tongue
in the dark, and it reminds me of rocks
hitting other rocks on a gravel road.

I can hear water running through the pipes,
and it makes me think of a creek
in the woods, but I can't remember the name

of the creek. I think I will call it
Ice Creek, because it is so cold,
or maybe New Nickel Creek.
It is a shiny creek.

I can hear my dad speaking sharply
to my big sister. His voice
won't let me go to sleep,

so I try to think about the gravel road
that leads to New Nickel Creek,
and finally my sister comes to bed.
She puts an extra blanket on me.

Deer Dream

When the deer in my dream
stops to rest,
she faces the wind.
She breathes a piece of the cold wind
and warms it up.
I think this deer
will live forever.
I will follow her tracks
in the snow of my dream
with my pockets full
of fresh leaves.
The deer is leaping!
Look at her white tail!
How can she run so fast
through the trees?
She is a runner without any home
except my dream.

Jay's River Walk

When Jay went to the river today,
he picked up a piece of quartz.
An eagle flew over his head,
so close he could hear the air
in its wings.
Then the eagle was gone.
Jay and his dad rode home
through a torrent of headlights,
leaving the river where it belonged.
They had leftover chili for supper
and didn't talk much.
Jay's dad took off his glasses
and rubbed his eyes.
The quartz glimmered in the lamplight
when Jay took it out of his pocket
to put it on the table
by his dad's bowl.

Ben Under the Blankets

Under the blankets,
Ben is the seed in a cherry.
His flashlight
lights up the ends of his fingers.
Under the blankets,
he shines the beam
on the hardest maze
in his puzzle book.
Under the blankets,
Ben's a bee in honeycomb,
a jigsaw piece fitting in.
Under the blankets,
without peeking,
he knows the treasures
lined up on the cold windowsill:
the paper frog,
a boy made of clay,
and a tiny glass deer.
Under the blankets,
Ben finds the path that leads to
the castle in the heart
of the forest.

Hammer and Nails Dream

In my dream
I went back to the beginning of our town,
and I saw people building it.
I saw the moms spreading blankets
out on the grass.
I saw the dads carrying pouches of nails,
hammering the houses up
around their windows.
I saw the kids picking plums
from the trees by the creek,
eating some,
pocketing some to take home.

I wanted to say hello
to the people building the beginning
of our town.
I wanted to help them.
When the sun got low,
I wanted to give them a flashlight,
but in my dream
flashlights hadn't been
invented yet.

Night Garden

The garden has stories to tell,
like the sunflower seeds
with giants inside them,
and the beans,
eager
to climb
the sky
like Jack's
beanstalk
beans.
The marigold seeds
are a little afraid of the dark
and don't want to hear
the dirt's stories about
things that died.

Tonight the whole garden
is deep in thought.
The round radish seeds
think peppery and red
round radish thoughts.
The cosmos seeds
plan to build
a house of flowers
where butterflies
come knocking at the door.
And the cucumber seeds,
because they can think
of nothing else,
dream all night
about the rain.

Name Dream

Your name lives in a house
with bright windows.
The wind carries your name
with the cottonwood seeds.
Your name clacks
like a smooth stone
knocking against other stones
in the cold waves of the lake.
Your name is a campfire
with tiger shapes in it.

Your name was walking in the night.
There was a long way to walk,
but your name got home.

Breathing

Everyone
breathing—
baby curled up on top of his blankets
breathing,
sister stretched out flat on her back
breathing,
the others rolling this way and that
breathing,
and the furnace click-click-clicks,
whooshes, and then the whole house is
breathing,
and a snowy wind wraps around the house
because the earth is
breathing, too.

44

Window Around the Moon

The crescent moon shines
through the trees,
through the breezy air,
the little squares
of window screen,
then the windowpane,
and the fingerprints
on the glass.
The moon shines
down, and the eye
lets the light
in—through cornea,
lens, and retina.
Then the optic nerve
carries the moon
all the way into the brain.
Two hundred and forty thousand miles
from the window,
the old, old moon
is shining in our minds.